The Princess and the Pea

Adapted by Eric Fein
Illustrated by Anthony Lewis

ISBN: 0-7853-4301-6

Long ago and far away there lived a lonely prince. He spent endless days traveling from kingdom to kingdom in hopes of finding a real princess to be his wife.

But every noble lady he met turned out to be unacceptable. It was not that the women were not beautiful or smart, for they were. It was that none of the women had those certain special qualities that made them real princesses. The prince would only marry a real princess.

The king and queen worried about their son and did their best to raise his spirits.

"I know!" said the king. "We will invite all the wonderful women from every kingdom to the palace for a festival."

The royal family held the festival as promised, and hundreds of young women came with the hopes of marrying the prince. But it was no use. The prince found something wrong with every one of them. They all returned home disappointed.

One night, a terrible storm fell over the kingdom. Thunder bellowed, and lightning lit up the sky for miles around. Among the few souls unfortunate enough to be caught in the downpour was a fair maiden on her way home. The young lady's carriage had lost a wheel.

"We shall seek shelter in that castle in the distance," the princess told her driver. "I'm sure they will help us."

They made their way to the castle through the rain and the mud. At the castle, the prince had been preparing for bed when he heard a knock at the door. Not being very sleepy, he thought he would answer the door himself.

"Forgive our intrusion, Your Highness," said the princess as she stood at the door, dripping wet. "I am a princess. My carriage has lost its wheel. My driver and I have no place to stay."

Despite her muddy, rain-soaked appearance, the prince liked this young woman and wanted to help.

"Of course you may stay here," the prince said. "Come, allow me to show you to the fireplace, where you may warm yourself before you catch a cold."

"Thank you. That is very kind of you," said the princess.

Then the queen said, "While you warm yourself by the fire, I shall oversee the preparations for your stay in our guest room."

"You are all so good to me," said the princess.

The queen was not convinced that the young lady was truly a princess. To find out, she devised a clever test.

The servants piled twenty mattresses, one on top of the other. Then they put twenty fine quilts, one over the other, on top of the twenty mattresses. So soft and lush was the bed that any ordinary person would sleep forever. But then the queen placed a small uncooked pea under the bottom mattress.

"If she is a princess, she'll get no comfort out of this bed. For only the delicate nature of a true princess will be able to feel the pea under all these layers," said the queen.

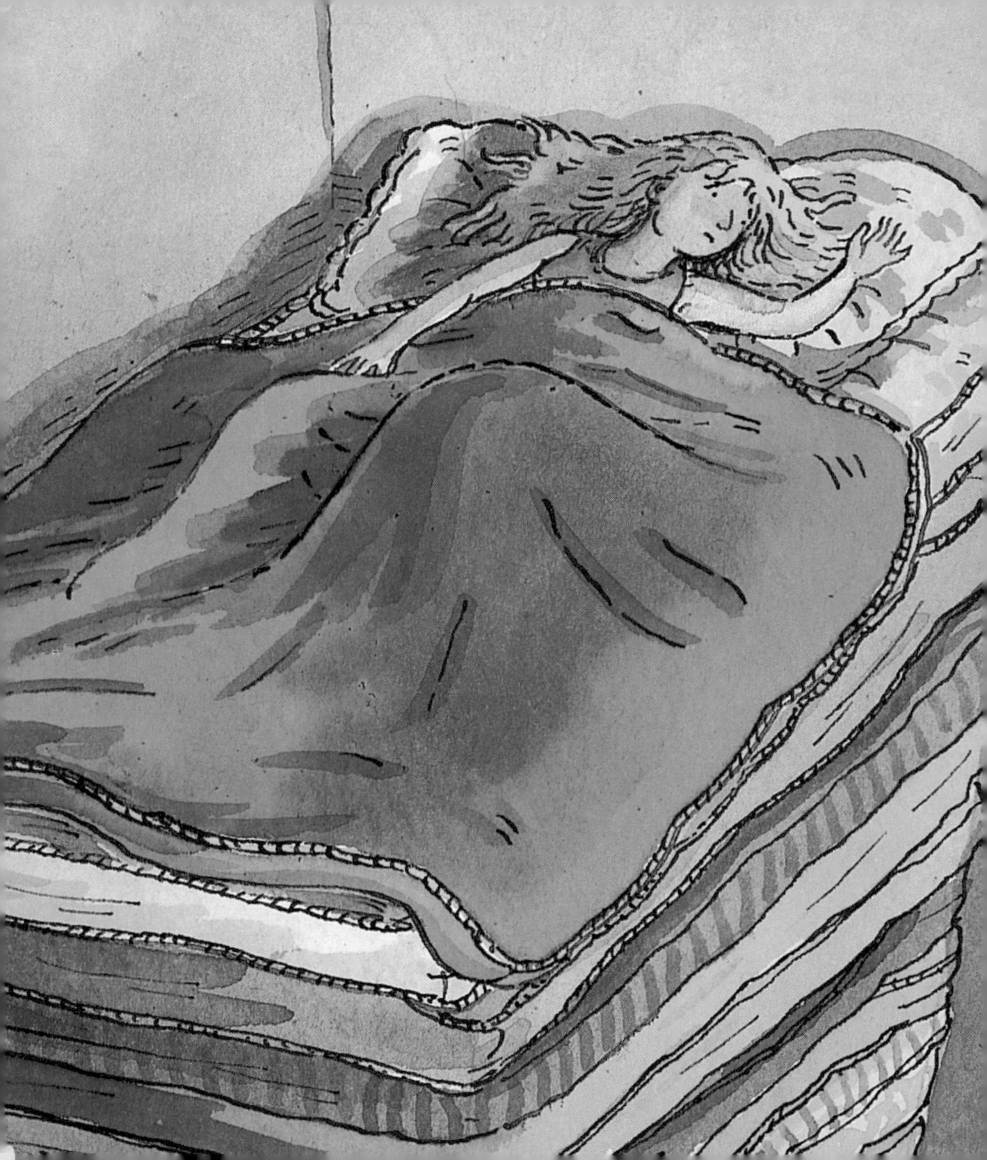

The prince and the princess talked for quite a while before turning in for the night. They enjoyed each other's company very much and went to bed smiling.

When the princess arrived at the guest room, she saw the exquisite bed for her to sleep in. The princess climbed into the bed and lay down. As soon as she did, she felt that something was not right. She turned onto her right side and then onto her left. She tried lying on her stomach, but that did not help. She even tried to sleep with her head on the opposite side of the bed and diagonally, too. Nothing worked.

"Oh, dear," said the princess. "How will I sleep in such an uncomfortable bed?"

To the princess, the night seemed as long as the beautiful bed was high.

The next morning, the princess joined the royal family for breakfast. The queen asked her how she had slept.

"The bed was truly lovely and soft," she said. "But I could feel something hard underneath it. It had me tossing all night. And guess what I found underneath the bottom mattress—a pea!" said the princess.

The queen whispered, "She is indeed a true princess."

The prince was happy, for he had fallen in love with the princess. He got down on one knee and proposed.

The princess agreed to marry the prince, for she had fallen in love with him, too. Then the prince and princess lived happily ever after.